Once Upon A Shabbos

Written by
Jacqueline Jules

Illustrated by
Katherine Janus Kahn

This **PJ BOOK** belongs to

PJ Library

JEWISH BEDTIME STORIES and SONGS

KAR-BEN
PUBLISHING

For Alan, Kevin, and Neal
— J.J.

To Evelyn and Sidney Ungar and Freda Schneider
who shop on this street in N.Y.,
and to my friend, Nancy Ungar Schneider
who brought me there.
—K.J.K.

Text © 1998 Jacqueline Jules
Illustrations © 1998 Katherine Janus Kahn

Kar-Ben Publishing
A division of Lerner Publishing Group, Inc.
241 First Avenue North
Minneapolis, MN 55401 U.S.A.

For updated reading levels and more information, look up this title at www.lernerbooks.com.

Library of Congress Cataloging-in-Publication Data

Jules, Jacqueline, 1956–
    Once Upon a Shabbos / Jacqueline Jules : illustrated by Katherine Janus Kahn.
        p.   cm.
    Summary: A bear keeps taking the honey needed for the Shabbos kugel, until
Grandma learns that he is lost and invites him to come to dinner.
    ISBN 978–1–58013–020–2 (hardcover)
    ISBN 978–1–58013–021–9 (pbk.)
    [1. Grandmothers—Fiction. 2. Sabbath—Fiction. 3. Jews—Fiction.
4. Bears—Fiction. 5. New York (N.Y.)—Fiction.]
I. Kahn, Katherine, ill. II. Title.
PZ7.J929470n 1998
[E]—dc21   98-24828

Manufactured in Hong Kong
2 — PN — 9/1/15

011622.7K2/B0755/A4

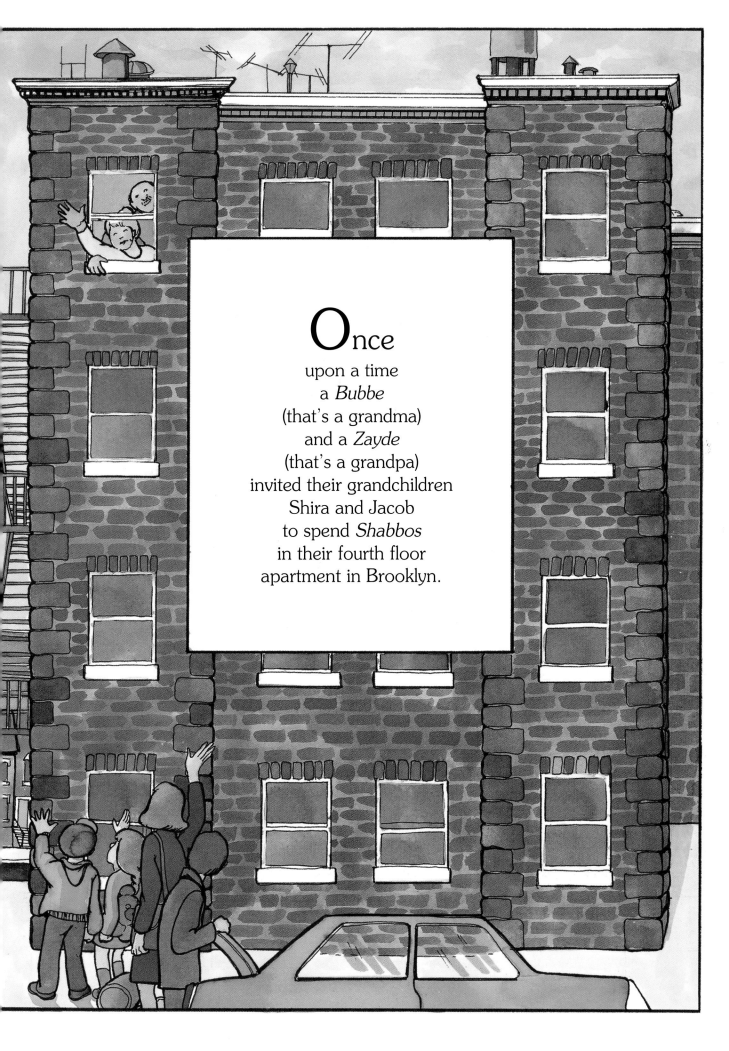

Once
upon a time
a *Bubbe*
(that's a grandma)
and a *Zayde*
(that's a grandpa)
invited their grandchildren
Shira and Jacob
to spend *Shabbos*
in their fourth floor
apartment in Brooklyn.

On Friday morning, the Bubbe went into the kitchen
to make her sweet Shabbos *kugel* (that's pudding).

She took out the noodles, the eggs, the pineapple, and the cinnamon. But when she went to the cupboard to get the honey, she saw the jar was empty.

"No honey!" she cried. "I must have honey for my Shabbos kugel."

She cupped her hands over her mouth and called, "Jacob, Jacob!"

Jacob came into the kitchen right away. 'What's up, Bubbe?"

"We have no honey to sweeten the Shabbos kugel. Please go down to the corner store and buy some, while I boil the noodles." Bubbe gave Jacob a little *gelt* (that's money), and he ran out of the apartment singing:

Honey, honey sweet as Shabbos!
Honey, honey sweet as Shabbos!

Jacob slid down four flights of stairs to the street

and skated three blocks to the corner store.

He paid for a jar of honey

and skated three blocks back to the apartment building.

But when he started up the stairs,

a great big bear jumped out at him and roared:

"Give me your honey, or I'll eat you up!"

Jacob looked at the bear and saw big, white teeth and long, pointy claws and decided he didn't want to argue with this bear. He handed over the honey and ran up the stairs as fast as he could.

"Bubbe," he cried. "Bubbe! A bear stole the honey!"

Bubbe couldn't believe what she was hearing. She put her hands on her hips and asked, "Are you *meshugah* (that's crazy)! There are no bears in Brooklyn. I guess I'll have to send your sister Shira."

She cupped her hands over her mouth and called, "Shira, Shira!"

Shira came into the kitchen right away. "What's up, Bubbe?"

"We have no honey to sweeten the Shabbos kugel. Please go down to the corner store and buy some, while I add the pineapple."

Bubbe gave Shira a little gelt, and she ran out of the apartment singing:

Honey, honey sweet as Shabbos!
Honey, honey sweet as Shabbos!

Shira walked down four flights
of stairs to the street,

and three blocks
to the corner store.

She paid for a jar of honey and walked three blocks back to the apartment building.

But when she started up the stairs, a great big bear jumped out at her and roared:

"Give me your honey, or I'll eat you up!"

Shira looked at the bear and saw big, white teeth and long, pointy claws and decided she didn't want to argue with this bear. She handed over the honey and ran up the stairs as fast as she could.

"Bubbe!" she cried. "Bubbe! A bear stole the honey!"

Bubbe couldn't believe what she was hearing. She put her hands on her hips and asked, "Are you meshugah? There are no bears in Brooklyn. I guess I'll have to send your Zayde."

She cupped her hands over her mouth and called, "Zayde, Zayde!" Zayde didn't come right away. He was older and walked slower. It took a few minutes for him to make it into the kitchen.

"*Vos iz*?" (that means what's the matter?) he asked Bubbe.

"We have no honey to sweeten the Shabbos kugel. Please go down to the corner store and buy some, while I beat the eggs."

So Zayde put a little gelt in his pocket and left the apartment singing:

Honey, honey sweet as Shabbos!
Honey, honey sweet as Shabbos!

Zayde walked down four flights of stairs to the street
and three blocks to the corner store.

He paid for a jar of honey and walked three blocks
back to the apartment building.

But when he started up the stairs, a great big bear jumped out and roared:

"Give me your honey, or I'll eat you up!"

Zayde looked at the bear and saw big, white teeth and long, pointy claws and decided he didn't want to argue with this bear. He handed over the honey and ran up the stairs as fast as he could.

"Bubbe," he cried. "Bubbe!
A bear stole the honey!"

Bubbe couldn't believe what she was hearing. She put her hands on her hips, and asked, "Are you meshugah? There are no bears in Brooklyn. I guess I'll have to get the honey myself."

She walked down four flights of stairs to the street and three blocks to the corner store.

She paid for a jar of honey and walked three blocks
back to the apartment building.

But when she started up the stairs

"Give
your
or
you

Well, let me tell you Bubbe was a *balabusta* (that's THE boss!).
She wasn't going to let anything interfere with her Shabbos dinner.

a great big bear jumped out at her and roared:

me honey, I'll eat up!"

She put her hands on her hips, looked the bear straight in the eye,
and said: "Bears don't live in Brooklyn."

"I know," said the bear in a very sad voice. "I'm lost." He plopped down on the bottom step and put his head in his paws. He looked so miserable that Bubbe couldn't help feel *rachmones* (that's compassion) in her heart.

"So tell me where you come from," Bubbe asked.

"From a storybook," said the bear.

"A storybook!" Bubbe said. "How wonderful! My grandchildren love stories. Why don't you come up and spend Shabbos with us. After dinner, you can tell us your story."

"Shabbos dinner!" exclaimed the bear. "I'd love to come to Shabbos dinner. What can I bring?"

"You can bring some honey," said Bubbe.

And Bubbe and the bear
climbed the four flights of stairs singing:

Honey, honey sweet as Shabbos!
Honey, honey sweet as Shabbos!

Honey, honey sweet as Shabbos!
Honey, honey sweet as Shabbos!